The Gingerbread Man

My First Reading Book

Story retold by Janet Brown
Illustrations by Ken Morton

ARMADILLO

A little old woman and man live alone in a tiny house. One day the woman decides to surprise her husband.

So she makes him a Gingerbread Man with eyes of chocolate buttons and a mouth of sugar-candy.

What does the little old woman do to surprise her husband?

But when the little old man arrives home, the Gingerbread Man leaps off the table and runs out the door.

"Come back!" cry the little old woman and man but the Gingerbread Man just laughs and sings,

"Run, run as fast as you can,

You can't catch me, I'm the Gingerbread Man!"

And they can't.

What does the Gingerbread Man do as soon as the little old man arrives home?

As the Gingerbread Man runs through a field, a cow calls to him,

"Stop, little man, I would like to eat you!"

But the Gingerbread Man just laughs and sings,

"I have run away from a little old woman and man,

And I can run from you, I can!

Run, run as fast as you can,

You can't catch me, I'm the Gingerbread Man!"

And the cow can't.

Who is the first animal to meet the Gingerbread Man?

As the Gingerbread Man runs through a stable, a horse calls to him,

"Stop, little man, I would like to eat you!"

But the Gingerbread Man just laughs and sings,

"I have run away from a little old woman and man, *and a cow,*

And I can run from you, I can!

Run, run as fast as you can,

You can't catch me, I'm the Gingerbread Man!"

And the horse can't.

Where does the Gingerbread Man meet the horse?

As the Gingerbread Man runs through a farm, a farmer calls to him,

"Stop, litlle man, I would like to eat you!"

But the Gingerbread Man just laughs and sings,

"I have run away from a little old woman and man,

and a cow,

and a horse,

And I can run from you, I can!

Run, run as fast as you can,

You can't catch me, I'm the Gingerbread Man!"

And the farmer can't.

Why does the farmer want to catch the Gingerbread Man?

As the Gingerbread Man runs through a wood, he sees a fox. Now the Gingerbread Man is so proud he thinks no one can catch him. So when the fox starts to run, he laughs and sings,

"I have run away from a little old woman and man,

and a cow,

and a horse.

and a farmer,

And I can run from you, I can!

Run, run as fast as you can,

You can't catch me, I'm the Gingerbread Man!"

But the fox just laughs and keeps running.

How many people are chasing the Gingerbread Man now?
(Clue: Read the song again!)

"What's so funny?" asks the Gingerbread Man.

"I like your song," says the fox.

And under his breath he starts to sing:

"Run, run as fast as you can!"

The Gingerbread Man is rather pleased. For a while he and the fox run side by side.

Suddenly a river rises up in front of them. The river is wide and the Gingerbread Man cannot swim. The litlle old woman and man and the cow and the horse and the farmer are catching up behind.

Why can't the Gingerbread Man cross the river?

"One clever fellow should always help another," says the fox.

"Climb up on my tail and I will lake you to the other side."

As they go into the water the Gingerbread Man turns to laugh at everyone on the bank.

"You can't swim but you see I can!

You can't catch me, I'm the Gingerbread Man!"

Can you guess why the fox is helping the Gingerbread Man to cross the river?

After a while the fox says,

"The water is getting deeper. Climb up on my back."

Then he says,

"The water is getting deeper. Climb up on my neck."

And then he says,

"The water is gelling deeper. Climb up on my nose."

And when he reaches the shore, the fox tosses his head and the Gingerbread Man flies into his mouth.

"Yummy!" says the fox.

And the Gingerbread Man says nothing at all.

Why do you think the Gingerbread Man says nothing at all?

Look carefully at the Gingerbread Men below.
Find four identical pairs and spot the odd one out.

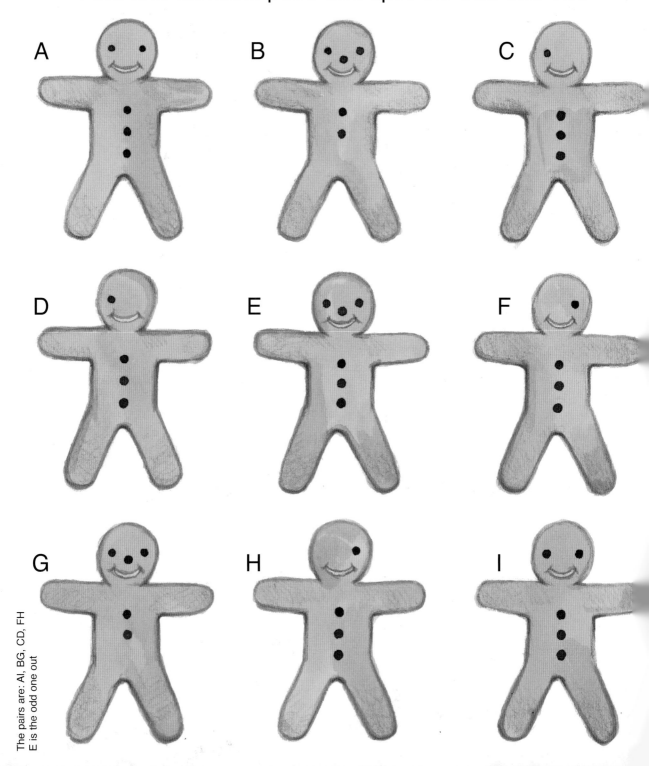

A B C

D E F

G H I

The pairs are: AI, BG, CD, FH
E is the odd one out